Text copyright © Roy Apps 1994
Illustrations copyright © Scoular Anderson 1994

First published in Great Britain in 1994
by Simon & Schuster Young Books
Campus 400
Maylands Avenue
Hemel Hempstead
Herts HP2 7EZ

Reprinted in 1994

Typeset in 15/23 pt Palatino by Goodfellow & Egan Ltd, Cambridge
Printed and bound in Portugal by Ediçoes ASA

British Library Cataloguing in Publication Data available.

ISBN: 0 7500 1477 6
ISBN: 0 7500 1478 4 (pb)

Roy Apps

𝕹igel the 𝕻irate

Illustrated by Scoular Anderson

SIMON & SCHUSTER
YOUNG BOOKS

Parte ye Firste
In Which
Aunt Etheline Forgets Something . . .

Aunt Etheline closed her eyes and settled back into the large, comfy seat of the aeroplane.

"Going on holiday is so terrifically exciting, isn't it dear?" she said to her nephew Nigel.

As they climbed steeply through the white clouds, Aunt Etheline began to develop a nagging feeling that she had forgotten something, but for the life of her she couldn't think what it was.

She checked her handbag for her passport, tickets, travellers' cheques and tummy-ache tablets; nothing seemed to be missing.

"I think I've forgotten something, but I don't know what it is," she explained to the air hostess.

"Why not have a nice cup of coffee?" suggested the stewardess.

"Oh, thank you. And I expect you'd like a glass of milk, wouldn't you Nigel?" she said turning to her nephew.

But Nigel's seat was empty. And suddenly Aunt Etheline knew what it was she had forgotten.

"Nigel!" she declared. "I've forgotten my nephew Nigel!"

Parte ye Second
In Which
Nigel Gets Very Cross . . .

To be fair to Aunt Etheline, it *was* very easy to forget Nigel. You see, Nigel was *quiet*. In fact he was so quiet that when you were with him you could hear a pin drop on to a pile of cushions on the other side of the room. He always shut doors behind him carefully; he never used the hall as a roller-skating alley; he never burped at meal times and the only films he ever watched on the telly were *silent* movies.

But now, as well as being quiet, he was very cross indeed. "Stupid, stupid Aunt! Forgetting to take me on holiday," he muttered to himself – silently, of course. And he threw his book – a very quiet sort of book called *Ninety Ways to Become a Nicer Nephew* – straight into the bin.

"I wish I could show her!" declared Nigel. "I wish I could teach Aunt Etheline a lesson!"

THUMP, THUMP, THUMP! came a sound behind him.

Nigel blinked and looked around.

BANG, BANG, BANG!

Someone was hammering on the front door.

He tip-toed through to the hall, opened the front door and came face to knee with a wooden leg.

"Cawww!!! Gibbering giblets! You look as wet as a deck mop and you've less meat on ye than that swine of a bosun had after I fed him to the sharks! What's ye name?" cried a voice so loud and so coarse it rattled the glass in the windows.

Nigel raised his head up . . . and up . . . and up – and found he was looking into the leathery, whiskery, scar-cheeked face of a pirate.

"My name," said Nigel, "is Nigel."

"Ha! That's no fault of yours," roared the pirate. He held out a scrawny hand. "*My* name's Cap'n Silas Bonegrinder. And this pesky creature," he added, pointing to the parrot on his right shoulder, "is Reginald."

"Silly billy!" croaked Reginald.

"I'm visitin' these parts," Cap'n Bonegrinder's grin was as welcoming as a crocodile's, "lookin' for an apprentice boy pirate."

Nigel had never dreamt of becoming a pirate. He had always fancied himself in a quiet job: as a museum attendant or a librarian perhaps. But he was still very cross with Aunt Etheline and he thought of just how much he'd like to teach her a lesson. If he became a pirate, that would certainly show her a thing or two!

"Yes! I'd like to become an apprentice boy pirate please," said Nigel brightly.

"Silly billy!" croaked Reginald. But Nigel didn't hear.

"Ye're a bit thin," said Cap'n Bonegrinder doubtfully. "I've seen more muscle on a cream cracker."

"Er . . . I only want to be an apprentice boy
pirate for about two weeks," added Nigel
quickly.

"Ha! A sort of holiday, d'ye mean?" asked
Cap'n Bonegrinder with a sneer.

"That's right!" said Nigel. "Just long
enough to teach my Aunt Etheline a lesson."

"Are ye ruthless and bloodthirsty?" asked Cap'n Bonegrinder.

"Er . . . I've never actually ever tried being ruthless and bloodthirsty," replied Nigel, "but I am very *quiet*."

"Hmmm . . ." Cap'n Bonegrinder looked thoughtful. "Have ye got a parrot?"

"No, but I have got a budgie – though he doesn't talk," replied Nigel.

"Silly billy!" croaked Reginald.

"Consider yourself an apprentice boy pirate," said Cap'n Bonegrinder. "Now pick up ye budgie and let's get down to the quay, for me ship *The Bloody Plunderer* sails on the midnight tide."

Parte ye Third
In Which
Nigel Gets Homesick . . .

The night sky was as dark as a dungeon and the night sea was as black as oil. Nigel slept peacefully in his hammock as *The Bloody Plunderer*, its timbers creaking like rusting hinges, made her way down to the seven seas.

Next morning, Nigel woke bright and early, full of excitement. He found Cap'n Bonegrinder in his cabin. "I'd like my breakfast, please," said Nigel.

"Silly billy!" croaked Reginald.

"Oh aye, ye breakfast." Cap'n Bonegrinder grinned slyly, from between a row of dirty, yellowing teeth which were as chipped and as crooked as old tombstones.

He placed a plate of ship's biscuits on the table. Nigel picked up the biggest biscuit and took a bite. It was as dry as sawdust, but that didn't worry Nigel half as much as the feeling that something tiny and leathery was crawling about under his tongue.

"Don't ye worry about that," roared Cap'n Bonegrinder. "Them's only weevils! Bite 'em in half with yer front teeth – that soon kills the little varmints – then spit 'em out." He gave Nigel a demonstration, and then burped as long and as loud as a plug hole.

"Excuse me," said Nigel, "but could you direct me to the lavatory, please." At least there, thought Nigel, I shall be able to find some peace and quiet.

The Cap'n took Nigel up on deck. "There's yer lavatory," he threw back his head with a gurgling laugh and pointed over the side to the shark-infested waters of the seven seas. "Only make sure you're not facing the wind!"

Later that morning,
Cap'n Bonegrinder said:
"It's about time you
started earning yer keep.
I've got a job for ye."

He pointed to the tall
mast that loomed above
them. "You're to climb
the rigging to the crow's
nest and look out for
passing ships,"
he instructed.

"Why?" asked Nigel.

"Silly billy!" croaked Reginald.

"So that we can plunder 'em of course!" bellowed Cap'n Bonegrinder. "What else d'ye think pirates do?"

Nigel didn't know, because he had only ever read books like *Ninety Ways to Become a Nicer Nephew*.

"Is plundering noisy?" he asked.

"Noisy? I should say it is," answered Cap'n Bonegrinder with glee. "What with the blood-curdling yells and hand-to-hand fighting and the screams of the passengers and crew as you make off with all their gold."

"Oh dear," thought Nigel, as he sat high up in the crow's nest, watching the sea leap and dip before him. His budgie huddled under his collar for warmth.

"If I shut my eyes, I won't see any passing ships, and then I won't have to go plundering them," thought Nigel. He closed his eyes tightly, and found they were full of tears.

"I wish I was back home," he sniffed. "I wish I'd never run away. I wish I'd never ever wanted to teach Aunt Etheline a lesson."

He picked up one of Cap'n Bonegrinder's empty bottles from the floor of the crow's nest and scribbled a sad little note:

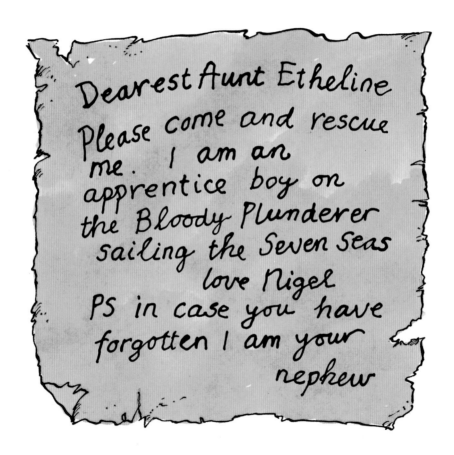

Dearest Aunt Etheline
Please come and rescue me. I am an apprentice boy on the Bloody Plunderer sailing the Seven Seas
love Nigel
PS in case you have forgotten I am your nephew

Then he popped the note into the bottle and threw it high and hard into the foaming waves beyond.

Down on the poop deck, Cap'n Bonegrinder was growing suspicious of Nigel's silence. He peered through his telescope and to his astonishment, saw the billowing sails of a Spanish galleon drifting over the horizon.

He hauled Nigel down from the crow's nest and pinned him against the capstan.

"Ye miserable cur!" he roared. "Didn't you see that Spanish galleon all laden with gold and doubloons? Why didn't ye shout out 'Ship Ahoy'?"

"Because I don't think I want to go plundering, if it's all the same to you, thank you very much," replied Nigel, politely. "You see, I'm a very *quiet* sort of boy."

"Don't want to go plundering!" Cap'n Bonegrinder waved a shining cutlass under Nigel's terrified nose. "Listen. If you don't

soon start behaving in an evil, ruthless and bloodthirsty fashion, I'll rip yer liver out and toss it to the sharks!"

"Can't you just take me home?" pleaded Nigel.

Cap'n Bonegrinder tossed back his head so that Nigel could see all the way up his hairy nostrils. He laughed a bloodthirsty laugh.

"Home? Home! What makes you think you're ever going home?"

"I only signed on for a two-week holiday," said Nigel, suddenly feeling very sick in the pit of his stomach.

"Silly billy!" croaked Reginald.

"All them who signs on with Cap'n Silas Bonegrinder signs on for the rest of their livin' days!" roared the Captain. "Now, as a punishment for being such a wet and weedy whinger, you can start scrubbing the poop deck with a toothbrush."

All day Nigel scrubbed. "I do hope Aunt Etheline comes and finds me," he sighed.

That night, just before he climbed into his hammock, Nigel asked Cap'n Bonegrinder, "Have you got a bedtime story I could read?"

"Ye can read this." Cap'n Bonegrinder slapped a book down in front of Nigel called *So You Want to Be a Bloodthirsty Pirate?*

Nigel peered at the first page through the swaying, smoky light of the oil lamp. This is what it said . . .

KEY STAGE ONE

HOW TO MOUNT
A MUTINY

"I say . . ." muttered Nigel, turning the page, "What a very *noisy* book!"

"Oooh. How very nasty . . ." he muttered, turning another page.

Nigel didn't look up until he had finished the whole of *Chapter One*. His eyes sparkled with excitement, then closed as he drifted off to sleep.

He knew exactly what he had to do.

Parte ye Fourth
In Which
Nigel Mounts A Mutiny . . .

At the crack of dawn, Nigel trotted up to the Cap'n Bonegrinder's cabin.

"Hey you!" he yelled at the Cap'n, who was so shocked he almost choked on the fried chicken giblets he was chewing for breakfast.

"I'm talking to you, Bonegrinder, you Pea-brained Old Pooper," Nigel shouted.

"Why you lily-livered landlubber!" roared the Cap'n and he leapt up from his table. "I'll -YEE-OWWW!"

And then very quickly indeed, he leapt down again.

"You can't move. I've screwed your wooden leg firmly to the deck," roared Nigel. "This is a mutiny. I read up on them in *So You Want to Be a Bloodthirsty Pirate* last night."

"Silly billy" croaked Reginald the parrot, only this time he said it to Cap'n Bonegrinder.

Nigel put on Cap'n Bonegrinder's black hat, belt and fancy waistcoat and made the Captain put on his own jumper and school tie. Then Reginald came and perched on Nigel's free shoulder.

Nigel marched Cap'n Bonegrinder up to the top deck.

"Now Bonegrinder," he ordered, "walk the plank!"

"Do you have to shout?" enquired Cap'n Bonegrinder meekly.

"Am I being noisy?" thundered Nigel, in a surprised tone. "So I am . . . so I am!" And he thought about it. "You know," he said, "it *is* rather fun being noisy, isn't it?"

And he bawled to Cap'n Bonegrinder at the top of his voice, "Now WALK THE PLANK!"

"I would if I could," replied the Cap'n, "but there isn't a plank to walk, ye miserable molly-coddled mutineer you!"

Nigel looked and saw that the Captain was right. There was no plank. Just a gap in the railings.

"Silly billy!" croaked Reginald.

"And I'm not telling ye where it is," chortled the Captain.

Nigel rushed down to the cabins below. He searched in every cupboard and in every hold, but all he found were bottles of rum and packets of parrot food.

Then, in the darkest corner of the Captain's cabin, he spotted a solid oak door secured with a padlock as big as a fist. Swinging Cap'n Bonegrinder's cutlass about his head, Nigel hacked off the padlock. The door creaked open to reveal – not just a plank, but a fully equipped radio station.

"Well I never!" muttered Nigel to himself in amazement. "I bet that's really noisy. I'd like a go on *that*!"

Then he remembered what he'd come for; so he grabbed the plank and dashed back up on deck.

"What are you doing with a radio station hidden away in your cabin?" he asked Cap'n Bonegrinder.

"That," explained Cap'n Bonegrinder grandly, "is my *pirate* radio station.* You wouldn't like it. The noise those rock groups make is worse than the blood-curdling yells of a hundred bloodthirsty pirates."

Suddenly, from the murky waters below there came a faint cry; "Ahoy there! Nigel, my pet!"

* If you don't know what a pirate radio station is, try asking someone really old – like your teacher, mum, dad, uncle, babysitter etc.

"Aunt Etheline!" exclaimed Nigel.

Still holding on to the plank, he swung round, quickly. The plank caught Cap'n Bonegrinder right behind his knobbly knee, knocking him overboard.

"Aaargh!" he cried.

"Man overboard!" cried Nigel. And he watched in horror as the Cap'n plummeted down towards the sea.

Thump!

Cap'n Bonegrinder landed, not in the water, but bang in the middle of Aunt Etheline's dinghy.

"Oh Nigel, my pet! I got your message! I'm so glad I've found you," cried Aunt Etheline and she wrapped her arms around the Captain and started planting wet kisses on his hairy cheek.

"She thinks the Captain's me! She's forgotten what I look like," sighed Nigel. "And after all, the Captain *is* wearing my clothes."

From the crow's nest, Nigel watched the dinghy slowly fade from sight over the horizon. Then he turned to Reginald.

"Come on," he said. "It's time we did something really noisy."

And he hurried down below to set up Cap'n Bonegrinder's pirate radio station.

Parte ye Fifth
In Which
Nigel Makes A Noise . . .

The bass beat pumps up and down like a piston, hammering away in Nigel's head until he's sure it will explode. He starts tapping his feet, nodding his head in time to the music.

"Hah! I'm through with being *quiet*," he yells down the microphone. "This one's for you, Captain Bonegrinder – and for you, Aunt Etheline – remember me? Your nephew Nigel! Come on you guys, get *real!*"

And so each and every night, Nigel plays the noisiest and loudest music in the world. He has millions of admiring listeners.

But none more devoted than Cap'n Silas Bonegrinder and his wife Etheline.

Look out for these other titles in the **Storybooks** series:

Look Out, Loch Ness Monster!
Keith Brumpton

For as long as he can remember, Kevin McAllister has longed to see the Loch Ness Monster. Then, one dark Scottish night, his dream comes true!

A Magic Birthday
Adele Geras
Illustrated by Adriano Gon

Maddy is delighted that Mr Osborne is going to do a conjuring trick at her birthday party. But she is very worried that there might not be a birthday cake . . .

Babybug
Catherine Storr
Illustrated by Fiona Dunbar

Tania's new baby brother has a baby alarm. "I wonder what people say about me when I'm in another room?" she wonders, and decides to change the baby alarm around.

Dreamy Daniel, Brainy Bert
Scoular Anderson

Daniel is always getting into trouble at school. But with the help of the brainy class mouse, Bert, Daniel learns to beat his day-dreaming habit.

Hopping Mad
Nick Warburton
Illustrated by Tony Blundell

Janey's little brother, Martin, is daft and completely useless. But he has one talent: he is very good at jumping around in a duvet cover. Janey has a wonderful idea – why not enter Martin for the big pillow race?

The Thing in the Sink
Frieda Hughes
Illustrated by Chris Riddell

Peter has always wanted a pet, but he never suspected that he would make friends with a long green slimy creature that lives in the bathroom basin!